Soccer in the British Isles

By
Mike Kennedy
with Mark Stewart

NORWOOD**H**OUSE **P**RESS

Norwood House Press, P.O. Box 316598, Chicago, Illinois 60631

For information regarding Norwood House Press,
please visit our website at: www.norwoodhousepress.com or call 866-565-2900.

Photo Credits:
  All interior photos provided by Getty Images.
Cover Photos:
  Top Left: Futera FZ LLC.
  Top Right: Phil Cole/Getty Images.
  Bottom Left: Ian Walton/Getty Images.
  Bottom Right: Futera FZ LLC.
The soccer memorabilia photographed for this book is part of the authors' collections:
  Page 10) Fletcher: Futera FZ LLC.
  Page 12) Dean: Gallaher Ltd.; Charles: A&BC Chewing Gum Ltd.; Charlton: Sporting Publications Ltd.; Best: A&BC Chewing Gum Ltd.
  Page 13) Keegan: Panini; Dalglish: Panini; Beckham: Brooke Bond & Co.; Rooney: Futera FZ LLC.

Designer: Ron Jaffe
Project Management: Black Book Partners, LLC
Editorial Production: Jessica McCulloch
Special thanks to Ben and Bill Gould

Library of Congress Cataloging-in-Publication Data
  Kennedy, Mike, 1965-
    Soccer in the British Isles / by Mike Kennedy with Mark Stewart.
      p. cm. -- (Smart about sports)
    Includes bibliographical references and index.
    Summary: "An introductory look at soccer teams and their fans in England,
  Ireland, Scotland, and Wales. Includes a brief history, facts, photos,
  records, and glossary"--Provided by publisher.
    ISBN-13: 978-1-59953-442-8 (library edition : alk. paper)
    ISBN-10: 1-59953-442-8 (library edition : alk. paper)
    1. Soccer--Great Britain--Juvenile literature. I. Stewart, Mark, 1960-
  II. Title.
    GV944.G7K46 2011
    796.3340941--dc22
                                          2010046319

© 2011 by Norwood House Press. All rights reserved.
No part of this book may be reproduced without written permission from the publisher.

Manufactured in the United States of America in North Mankato, Minnesota.
170N-012011

Contents

Where in the World? 5
Once Upon a Time 6
At the Stadium 9
Town & Country 10
Shoe Box 12
Can't Touch This 14
Just For Kicks 17
On the Map 18
Stop Action 20
We Won! 22
Soccer Words 24
Index 24
Learn More 24

Words in **bold type** are defined on page 24.

Scotland's players jump for joy after a goal.

Where in the World?

The British Isles are the birth place of soccer. The game began in England more than 150 years ago. It spread to Scotland, Ireland, and Wales. Today, millions of kids dream about playing soccer in the British Isles.

Once Upon a Time

The world's first soccer **league** started in England in 1863. Today, the 20 best teams in this part of the world compete in the Premier League. The games usually are played on the weekends.

Fans watch English star Stanley Matthews during a 1943 game.

Manchester fans are proud of their team.

At the Stadium

One of the most famous stadiums in the British Isles is Old Trafford. It is home to the Manchester United team. Old Trafford is over 100 years old.

Town & Country

The best players in the Premier League play for two different teams. In 2010, Darren Fletcher starred for Manchester United in England. Fletcher was born in Scotland. He played for Scotland's **national team**, too.

Darren Fletcher makes a pass for Manchester United.

Shoe Box

The sports collection on these pages belongs to the authors. It shows some of the top soccer stars from the British Isles.

Dixie Dean
Forward • England
Dixie Dean was England's first sports hero.

John Charles
Midfielder • Wales
John Charles was known for his powerful leg and good sportsmanship.

Bobby Charlton
Midfielder • England
Bobby Charlton could attack the goal from any part of the field.

George Best
Forward • Northern Ireland
Soccer fans around the world loved George Best.

Kevin Keegan

Striker • England
Kevin Keegan played with great skill and courage.

Kenny Dalglish

Striker • Scotland
Kenny Dalglish was at his best when playing for a championship.

David Beckham

Midfielder • England
David Beckham was a master of the **free kick**.

Wayne Rooney

Striker • England
At 17, Wayne Rooney became the youngest player to score for England.

13

Can't Touch This

The only players allowed to touch the ball with their hands are goalkeepers. They can catch and throw the ball. But they may only do so when they are inside the **penalty box**.

Goalkeeper Rachel Brown of England looks for an open teammate.

David Beckham of England takes a corner kick.

Just For Kicks

Watching soccer is more fun when you know some of the rules:

- A corner kick happens when the defense knocks the ball out of its own end.

- The kicking team puts the ball in play from the corner.

- The ball must be placed touching the corner's round line.

- The defenders must stand back 30 feet (9.1 meters).

On the Map

There are soccer leagues all over the British Isles.

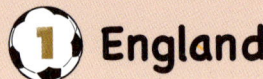 England

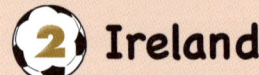 Ireland

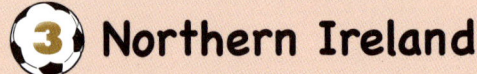 Northern Ireland

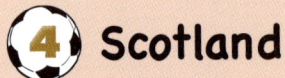 Scotland

 Wales

1 England

Many countries have their own soccer stamps!

19

Stop Action

Roy Keane of Ireland heads the ball.

Every player on a team wears a different number.

A soccer ball weighs about one pound (0.45 kilograms).

Soccer players pull their socks up to their knees.

We Won!

The British Isles have some of the best teams in the world!

Men's Soccer	World Cup Champion	Olympic* Champion
England	1966	1900, 1908, & 1912

Women's Soccer	European Championship Third Place
England	1984 & 2009

* The Olympics are a worldwide sports competition. Soccer has been part of the Olympics since 1900.

English players celebrate a goal in 2009.

Soccer Words

FREE KICK
A shot given to a team after a foul has been called.

LEAGUE
A group of teams that compete against each other.

NATIONAL TEAM
A team made up of players from the same country.

PENALTY BOX
The large box outlined in front of the goal.

Index

Beckham, David	13, **13**, **16**
Best, George	12, **12**
Brown, Rachel	**15**
Charles, John	12, **12**
Charlton, Bobby	12, **12**
Dalglish, Kenny	13, **13**
Dean, Dixie	12, **12**
Fletcher, Darren	10, **10**, **11**
Keane, Roy	**20**
Keegan, Kevin	13, **13**
Matthews, Stanley	**7**
Rooney, Wayne	13, **13**

Photos are on **bold** numbered pages.

Learn More

Learn more about the World Cup at www.fifa.com

Learn more about men's soccer at www.mlssoccer.com

Learn more about women's soccer at www.womensprosoccer.com